BIGGER BITES FOR
NIBBLES
BIGGER READERS!

QUACK! QUACK!

Jack can make a special sound
like a duck! Can you make it, too?
Can you help Jack rescue the little
duck from the duck hunter?

RIF
Reading is
Fundamental

MORE NIBBLES TO SINK YOUR TEETH INTO!

QUACK! QUACK!

Help Jack save the ducks!

James Moloney

Illustrated by Stephen Michael King

RUNNING PRESS
KIDS
PHILADELPHIA·LONDON

For Jock Grant. *J.M.*
For Herbal. *S.M.K.*

First published by Penguin Group (Australia),
a division of Pearson Australia Group Pty Ltd, 2004
First published in the United States
by Running Press Book Publishers, 2007.

Printed in China

9   8   7   6   5   4   3   2   1
Digit on the right indicates the number of this printing

Library of Congress Control Number: 2006929404
ISBN-13: 978-0-7624-2933-2
ISBN-10: 0-7624-2933-X

Original design by Karen Trump and Melissa Fraser,
Penguin Group (Australia).
Additional design for this edition by Frances J. Soo Ping Chow
Typography: New Century School Book

This book may be ordered by mail from the publisher.
Please include $2.50 for postage and handling.
But try your bookstore first!

This edition published by Running Press Kids, an imprint of
Running Press Book Publishers
2300 Chestnut Street
Philadelphia, PA 19103-4371

Visit us on the web!
www.runningpress.com

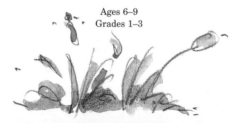

Ages 6–9
Grades 1–3

Instructions for Reading This Story

To read this story properly, you have to make a special sound. This is how you do it.

First, wet the palm of one hand with your tongue. Use lots of spit. (Hold your hand flat, or the spit will run off.) Now get your mouth ready. Begin by pushing your lips out as far they will go. Make sure your lips are held tightly together. Bring your hand up close to your mouth. Press your lips firmly into the wet palm. Now, blow sharply through your lips. It works best if you turn a little towards your thumb. If the

Quack

noise sounds rude, then you are not doing it properly.

Try again.

If the noise sounds a bit like a duck, then congratulations! That is just how it should sound. You are ready to read this story.

Chapter One

Jack was always the first one in his house to wake up. His two sisters liked to sleep on and on, for hours. What a waste! Jack couldn't wait to start each day. But he felt lonely eating breakfast by himself. Sometimes he would

stay in bed and listen for
the sounds of his sisters
stirring. Then he would get
up and have breakfast.

One cold Sunday morn-
ing, he snuggled under the
blankets. There was no one
to have breakfast with yet.
The girls were taking
forever to wake up.
A train rattled by on
the tracks at the

end of his street. Inside the
house, there were still no
footsteps, still no creaking
of bed springs.

But what was that? Jack had left his window open just a crack, and a sharp squawking noise had just sneaked through the gap. He waited. Yes, there it was again.

"Ducks," he said to himself. That was strange. He had never heard
the ducks so early in
the morning.

No, it's not time for our special sound just yet.

Chapter Two

Jack slipped out of bed
and went to the window.
He loved the view from
his window. Most children
can only see houses or
roads from their bedrooms.
Jack looked out onto a
huge park.

That morning, a thick
grey mist hung like milky
porridge around the
trees and over the pond
in the middle of the park.
The mist hid his view of
the ducks.

Sometimes he saw people walking their dogs in the park, but the cold had kept them away this morning.

Everything was still and silent. Then he heard that squawk again. Yes, it was definitely a duck.

He was out of bed already now. Sisters or no sisters, it was time to start the day. He dressed quickly in long pants and his warmest sweater, then hurried downstairs to the back door.

Jack had his own private entrance to the park. It

wasn't a gate. It was a hole
in the hedge he had made
himself. He knew every inch
of this park, every path,
every tree.

He hurried to the edge of the large pond. Out in the middle, he could see one duck, then two, three, four. They were barely moving.

Just like my sisters, he
thought. The same squawk
broke the morning silence
again.

But it wasn't coming from the middle of the pond. It was coming from the shore, from among the reeds and bushes hidden by the mist.

Sorry, be patient a little longer, it's still not time for our special sound.

Chapter Three

Jack went to investigate.
He had only taken a few
steps, when the mist rose
gently on a breath of breeze.
Now he could see a man,
crouching at the water's
edge. He was rather plump
and his grey hair made

him seem old. He put something to his lips and blew.
A duck's *quack* called across
the water.

Jack came closer, until
he was only a few feet away.
"How did you make that
sound?" he asked.

The man turned around
quickly. When he saw
Jack was only a little boy,
he relaxed. In fact, he
smiled. It was a smart,
unfriendly smile.

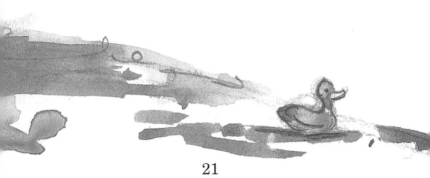

"See," he said, holding up something that looked like a whistle. He blew on it. Instead of a shrill peep, like the blast from a referee's whistle, out came another duck's *quack*.

"My grandfather made
this duck whistle. You can't
buy one as good as this in
the shops."

He blew on it again and this time the *quack* was answered. A little duck had come from the middle of the pond. The man blew again. The real duck quacked in reply and came closer.

The man stayed carefully hidden. He blew on that strange whistle again.

Quack

The duck came closer still. Jack didn't guess what he was up to, until it was too late. The man moved like lightning. His hand flashed

out through the reeds and
caught the little duck
around its neck. As Jack
watched in amazement, the
duck was stuffed roughly
into a canvas bag. Then a

string was tied tightly around the top.

The duck quacked in protest.

But, no, it's still not time for our duck sound.

Quack

Chapter Four

When Jack saw what the man had done, he was angry. "Hey! You can't do that," he cried.

The man didn't answer. He was already walking away along the path. Jack chased him. Luckily, the

man had a large and heavy
stomach, so he couldn't
walk very quickly. Jack
caught him easily.

This time, the man
turned around. "What do
you want?" he asked rudely.

"I want you to let that
duck go," said Jack. "It lives
here, in this pond. You
can't take him away. He'll
be lonely without the
other ducks."

"You don't need to worry.

He won't be lonely for long,"

said the man, as he held up

32

the bag. "By lunchtime he will be making friends with some nice potatoes. They can go swimming together in some gravy." Then he smiled and licked his lips.

"You can't *eat* him!"
cried Jack.

"Oh, yes, I can. Duck is my favorite food. Too bad this one is so small. I was hoping for a big juicy one. Now, excuse me. I have to get home and put the oven on."

Inside the bag, the little duck let out another angry *quack*.

Not long now. We will need that special sound, very soon.

Chapter Five

Jack had to save the little duck. But what could he do? The man was three times his size. By the time he ran home to fetch his dad, the man and the duck would both be gone.

Jack watched the man as

he turned away from the
pond. The railway line
blocked the way out of the
park on one side. He would

have to take the path
through the trees. Jack
knew that path. It wound
round like a snake. He

knew a quicker way, and
before he had finished making up his mind, his feet
were already running.

He hurried through the
trees. He stomped madly

through the garden beds. If
the gardeners had seen
him, they would have shout-
ed angrily. But they were
still asleep, like the rest of
the world. Jack was puffing

by now, but he knew he was
ahead of the man and the
little duck. He pushed his
way through the bushes
until he was close to the
path again. Just in time,
too, because he could hear

heavy footsteps.

What was he going to do now? His first plan was to jump out and snatch the bag. No, the path was wide and the man would see him coming. He needed to trick him somehow. What could he do?

At that moment, the poor little duck quacked loudly from inside the bag.

It was enough to give Jack an idea.

Get ready. We are very close.

Chapter Six

Jack quickly wet his hand
with his tongue. In fact, he
slobbered all over his palm.

Then he pushed his lips out, pressed them hard into the little pool he had made and blew a sharp blast of air. Out came a perfect duck sound. Just like this . . .

Okay. NOW!

The man stopped walk-
ing. Jack could just see him
through a tiny space
between the bushes. He
blew hard down into his wet
palm again.

Right. DO IT AGAIN!

Quack

The man looked closely at the bag in his hand. No, it hadn't come from the little duck he had captured.

Jack had to make the

man think it was a really
big duck, hidden in the
bushes. He took a deep
breath and blew as hard as
he could.

Time for a really BIG ONE!

It worked. The man took the duck whistle from his pocket and moments later, there was the squawk. Jack replied right away.

Again. Not so loud this time.

Quack

The man came closer, leaving the path now. Jack backed away with his lips still pushed into his hand.

It was time for the second part of his plan. This bit of the garden was overgrown with thin, curling vines. He snapped a vine from his left side. He snapped a piece from his right. He tied them quickly together with a strong knot.

By now, the man was very close. He was still hidden, but the squawking of his

duck whistle came from

only a few feet away.

Jack coaxed him on with

Quack

one last blast of his own
duck sound.

Last one. NOW!

Quack

He had barely finished, when the man leapt forward, hoping to grab a big, fat duck. But there was no duck. He broke through the bushes and all he saw was Jack.

The man's face crinkled in anger. "You again!" he cried. He took one more hurried step. . . .

It was his last. The vines
cut across his shins and
over he went, like a huge
tree chopped down in
the forest. As he fell, the
bag dropped from his hand.
Something else fell free,
too. In an instant, Jack
snatched them both up
and he was off.

Chapter Seven

Jack didn't follow any of the paths back to the pond. He had his own special ways, so the man couldn't catch him. In fact, the first the man even saw of Jack was when he reached the muddy edge of the pond.

Jack quickly untied the string that sealed the little duck inside.

"Hey, don't let it go!" the man called.

It was too late. Jack opened the bag and held it upside down. The duck fell into the water with a splash. Then, with a quick

flap of its wings, it took off
to join its friends in the
middle of the pond.

By then, the angry man
had puffed his way along
the path to where Jack
stood. "It's no use," he said.
"I'll catch another one next
week, you know."

Jack smiled and took
something out of his
pocket. He held it up
for the man to see. It
was the duck whistle. "You
won't be able to catch one
without this," he said.

"Here. That's mine. Give it to me!" The man reached forward suddenly, trying to grab the duck whistle.

Jack was too quick for
him. He took two steps to
the edge of the pond and
threw the duck whistle as
hard as he could. He had
never thrown anything so
far. It flew out over the
water. On and on it went,
until at last it landed, plop,

among the ducks. There it
sank, leaving a single bubble to show where it had
been. Then the bubble
popped. The man would
never get it back now.

"But it was the best duck
whistle in the world," the
man said. "There will never

be another one like it." He
seemed ready to cry.

Jack didn't care. He was
glad no more ducks would
be tricked by that whistle.
He didn't want them to end
up swimming in gravy,
instead of this pond.

"How am I going to call the
ducks now?" the man wailed.

Jack thought for a
minute. There was a way.
He was about to spit in his

hand, then stopped himself.
No, this was one secret he
would keep to himself.

"These ducks aren't for
eating. Even if you buy
another duck whistle, I

will hear you. I live in that house, there," Jack said, pointing at his bedroom window. "If I see you trying to catch any more ducks, I'll tell the police."

Jack turned and walked off. He climbed through the hole in the hedge. When he looked back, he saw the man slowly walking away. His shoulders were drooped and his hands were stuck in his pockets.

Jack was sure that the man would never come back, but he would keep a watch for him, all the same.

He opened the back door and there were his sisters.

"Where have you been, Jack? We got up early, so we could have breakfast with you."

Jack answered them with a noise. You know what noise it was,

a duck sound! Then he
sat down between his wide-
eyed sisters and told them
everything.

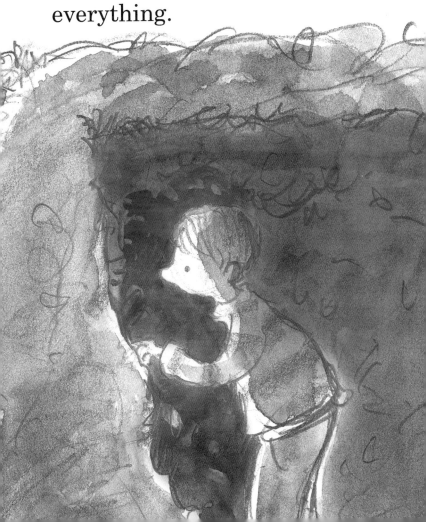

One Last Instruction for Readers of This Story

*You've got spit
on your palms. Yuck.
That's disgusting!*

*PLEASE WASH YOUR
HANDS THIS MINUTE!*

James Moloney

When I was in Paris one time, I saw two old men catching pigeons near a famous church called Sacré Coeur. My French friend told me that they would take the pigeons home and eat them. Later, I read about duck whistles in America. Some are hundreds of years old. They have been passed down from father to son over many generations. But when it comes to making noises with a wet palm, well . . . sometimes I was a naughty boy at school. I made noises like that at my teacher once, pretending that I was a duck. She spanked my bottom!

Stephen Michael King

I'm often awake early. My daughter and Milli (our new dog), are usually up too. Quietly, we wake up Muttley (our old dog) and jump into our beach van. Then we drive towards the coast. We live in a rural area, so the short drive is often haunting and misty. Sometimes the beach is rugged and windswept, other times it's calm with perfect glassy waves. We return at sunrise, long before the rest of our family is out of bed.

HUNGRY FOR MORE?

HAVE A NIBBLE!